I'M SMART!

KATE & JIM McMULLAN

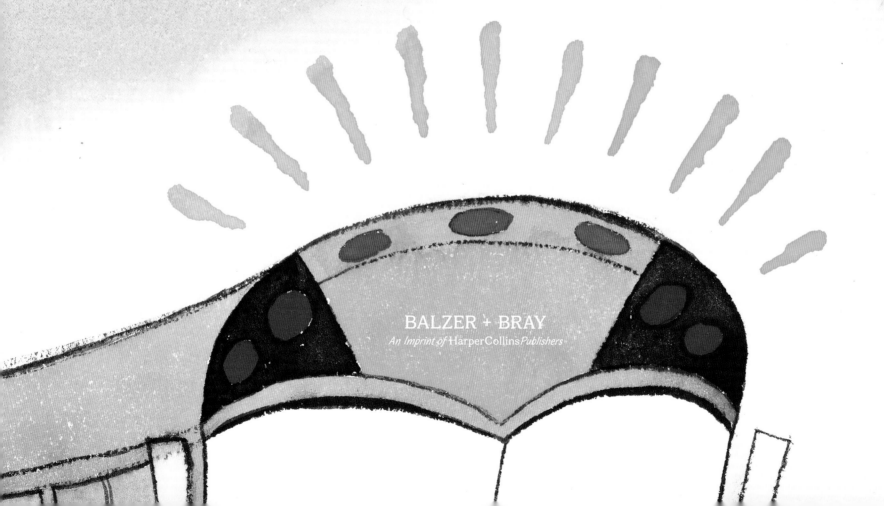

BALZER + BRAY
An Imprint of HarperCollins Publishers

I'm Smart!
Text copyright © 2017 by Kate McMullan
Illustrations copyright © 2017 by Jim McMullan
All rights reserved. Manufactured in China.
No part of this book may be used or reproduced in any manner whatsoever
without written permission except in the case of brief quotations embodied in
critical articles and reviews. For information address HarperCollins Children's Books,
a division of HarperCollins Publishers, 195 Broadway, New York, NY 10007.
www.harpercollinschildrens.com

Library of Congress Control Number: 2016941965
ISBN 978-0-06-244923-8

The artist used watercolor to create the illustrations for this book.
17 18 19 20 21 SCP 10 9 8 7 6 5 4 3 2 1
❖
First Edition

For our grandson, Arthur James Abramson,
and for school bus drivers everywhere

A busload of thanks to the inspiring men and women who agreed to talk
to me about driving a school bus: Henry Atwood of Stillwater, MN;
Charmaine Barr of Falls Church, VA; Imogene Knight of N. Manchester, IN;
Lila Sue Riley of Rolla, MO; and Don Worden of Harrisburg, PA.

Thanks to my friends who put me in touch with the drivers: Sally Cook, Bethany
Hall, Eileen Hurley, Stephanie Oppenheimer, Donna Williamson, and John Worden.

We're grateful to the HarperCollins team: Alessandra Balzer, Kelsey Murphy,
Dana Fritts, Ellice Lee, and Kathryn Silsand.

Thank you, Pippins: Holly McGhee, Heather Alexander, Elena Giovinazzo,
Michael Steiner, and that smart cookie, Courtney Stevenson.

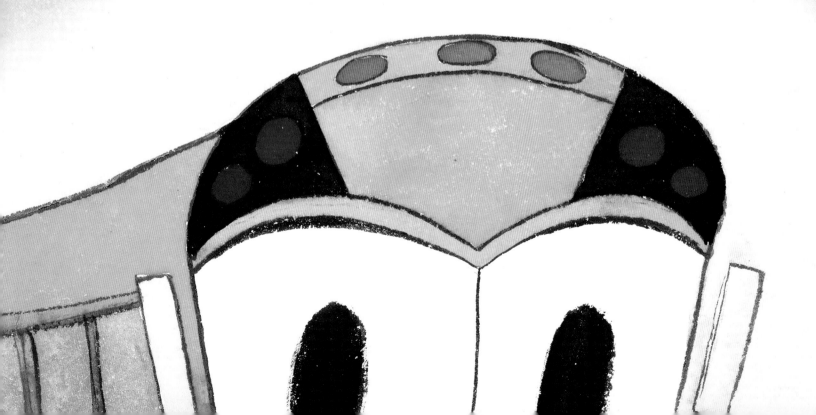

MONSTER TRUCK,

able to HALT TRAFFIC with the FLICK of a SWITCH.

STOP

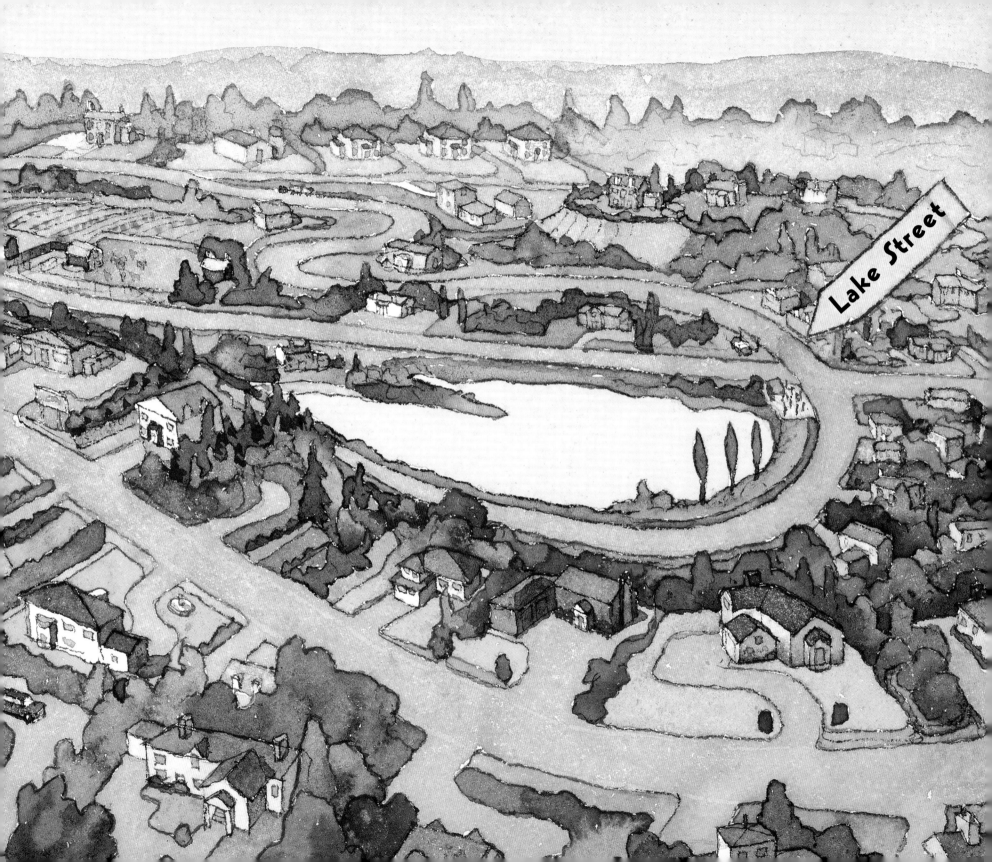

RED LIGHTS? FLASH! FLASH! FLASH!

Stop paddle?

EVERYBODY STOP!

And don't move till I quit flashing!

DAISY MOE MINNIE ROCKY BO

Next stop, LAKE STREET!

Here come the cops.

Who has a DOG? Who has a SNAKE?

Our turn. Let's go!

Oh no—bump coming up!

TA-DAH!
Got you to SCHOOL! On time, too.
Pat myself on the back . . .
er, roof.

Have a super day, kids!
After school, I'll be waiting right here.

Who am I?

Your SCHOOL BUS,

that's who!

THE END